Ellie the Evergreen

Warren Publishing House, Inc.

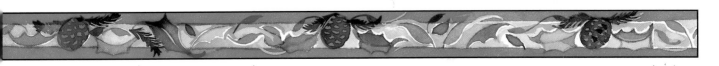

Warren Publishing House, Inc., P.O. Box 2250, Everett, WA, 98203, 1-800-334-4769.

Printed in Hong Kong by Mandarin Offset.
First Edition   10 9 8 7 6 5 4 3 2 1

Warren, Jean
Ellie the Evergreen/by Jean Warren; illustrated by Gwen Connelly; activity illustrations by Barb Tourtillotte. — 1st ed. — Everett, WA: Warren Publishing House, Inc., © 1993.

32 p.:ill.

Activity suggestions included (p.19-32).

1. Creative activities. 2. Seasons — Handbooks, manuals, etc. 3. Ecology — Handbooks, manuals, etc. 4. Trees — Handbooks, manuals, etc.

I. Connelley, Gwen.   II. Tourtillotte, Barb   III. Title.

92-62825
ISBN 0-911019-67-7

372.5

[E]

Warren Publishing House, Inc. would like to acknowledge the following activity contributor:

Debbi Jones, Richland, WA

Ellie the Evergreen

By Jean Warren

Illustrated by Gwen Connelly
Activity Illustrations by Barb Tourtillotte

It was fall. The trees in the park were busy changing into their new coats.

Soon the park was filled with the colors of yellow, red, gold, and brown.

All of the trees were excited and happy — all except Ellie.

Ellie was an evergreen tree. No matter how hard she wished to be colorful, her coat of needles stayed green.

The people in town came to the park to admire the beautiful coats on the other trees.

The squirrels played in their colorful leaves. The children danced under their branches.

Everyone said "Ooh!" and "Ahh!"

Ellie was sad. No one looked at her at all.

Soon the days grew shorter, and the nights grew colder.

The winds began to blow and the leaves began to fall off the trees.

One by one, the wind sent them twirling to the ground.

As the other trees lost their leaves, the people in town began to notice Ellie the Evergreen.

The squirrels ran up and down her trunk and played in her warm branches when it was cold.

And when the first snow fell, everyone admired her beauty.

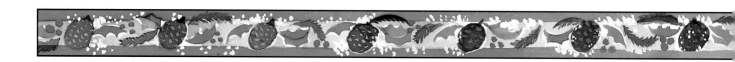

One day the townspeople came to the park and placed colorful lights on Ellie's branches.

When the lights were turned on, everyone smiled and said "Ooh!" and "Ahh!"

There was no doubt about it — Ellie was now the most beautiful tree in the park!

Everyone was happy for Ellie, even the other trees. They knew that fall was their season and that winter was Ellie's season.

Like the trees, we all have our season.

All we have to do is wait.

Fall Fun

Pressed Leaves

Brighten a window with this creation!

1. Place a sheet of waxed paper on top of a towel.

2. Arrange fall leaves on the waxed paper and then sprinkle Crayon Shavings on top of the leaves.

3. Cover the leaves and crayons with another piece of waxed paper, and place another towel on top.

4. Ask an adult to help you iron over the towel. With the iron, press hard for about 15 seconds. The wax in the paper and Crayon Shavings will melt together and seal in the pressed leaves.

5. Tape your pressed leaves in a window and watch them shine in the light.

You Will Need
two towels • waxed paper • fall leaves • crayon shavings • an iron

Crayon Shavings
Use a cheese grater to grate crayon pieces into shavings.

Dried Leaf Mosaic

Make a colorful design with crushed leaves!

1. Sort fall leaves into piles of different colors. For example, make a pile of yellow leaves, a pile of orange leaves, a pile of red leaves, and a pile of brown leaves.

2. Crumble the leaves in each pile into small pieces.

3. Brush a thin layer of glue all over a piece of cardboard.

4. Arrange the leaf pieces in a pattern, such as a row of red leaf pieces, two rows of yellow leaf pieces, four rows of orange leaf pieces, and so on.

5. Glue the pattern on the cardboard.

6. Repeat the pattern and watch your beautiful mosaic appear.

For More Fun

• Use your leftover leaf pieces to make a face on a paper plate. Use larger leaf bits to make the hair.

You Will Need
colorful fall leaves • glue • a brush • a piece of cardboard

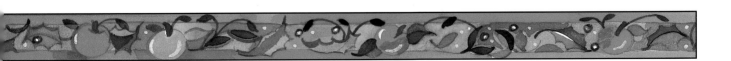

Super Leaf Print

1. Arrange fall leaves on a piece of newspaper.

2. Paint the fronts of the leaves with red, yellow, and orange paint.

Decorate your wall with a bright, bold picture!

You Will Need

fall leaves • newspaper • red, yellow and orange paint • brushes • cardboard • black construction paper

3. Carefully move your leaves to a piece of clean cardboard, arranging them however you wish.

4. Lay a piece of black construction paper on top of the leaves and press your hands over the top of the paper.

5. Carefully pick up the black paper, and you'll have a beautiful colored print of your leaves.

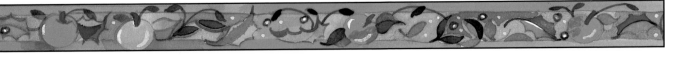

Dancing Leaf Puppet

These funny leaf puppets can dance to your favorite fall songs!

1. Use a felt-tip marker to draw a face on a large leaf.

2. Tape four yarn pieces to the back of a cardboard square, two for arms and two for legs.

You Will Need

one large leaf • four smaller leaves • a felt-tip marker • tape • four 2-inch pieces of yarn • a 4-inch-square of cardboard • glue • a tongue depressor or a craft stick

3. Glue the large leaf to the front of the cardboard square.

4. Tape a smaller leaf to the end of each of the yarn pieces.

5. Tape a tongue depressor to the back of the cardboard square for a handle.

6. Make your puppet dance and sway to your favorite songs.

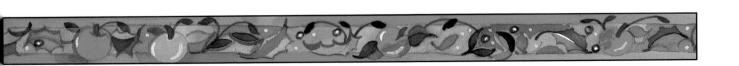

Leaf Show-Off

1. Choose two or three leaves and lay them in a plastic lid.

2. Sprinkle glitter or Paper Confetti around the edges of the leaves.

3. Ask an adult to help you cut the rim off another plastic lid so that it will fit snugly inside the first lid.

4. Place the rimless lid on top of the leaves and snap it in place.

Frame your favorite leaves in this simple holder.

5. Use a hole punch to make a hole at the top of your leaf frame. (Or ask an adult to use a craft knife to make the hole for you.)

6. String a ribbon through the hole and tie it to make a loop. Hang your leaf frame in a window.

You Will Need

two clear-plastic lids (both the same size) from coffee cans or margarine tubs • scissors • fall leaves • glitter or Paper Confetti • a hole punch • ribbon

Paper Confetti

Instead of glitter, you can make Paper Confetti by using a hole punch to punch out circles from colored construction paper.

Winter Fun

Frost Pictures

Decorate your wall with pictures touched by Jack Frost!

1. Cut out pictures from used holiday cards and glue them onto a piece of construction paper.

2. Brush some Secret Salt Mixture over the pictures.

3. Watch the pictures turn into a frosty scene as the water dries and shiny crystals appear.

For More Fun

• Frost pictures can be made with any pictures, even those you color yourself.

You Will Need

used holiday greeting cards • scissors • glue • construction paper • a brush • Secret Salt Mixture

Secret Salt Mixture

Ask an adult to help you make this crystal mixture. Mix one part Epsom salts to one part boiling water. Let the mixture cool before using.

Snow Scene

This snow scene is so beautiful and so simple!

1. Turn a plastic lid upside down and fill it with Sticky Dough.

2. Push some small pine cones into the dough so that they stand up.

3. Ask an adult to help you spray your pine-cone scene with snow spray, and watch as your pine cones turn into beautiful evergreen trees covered with snow.

For More Fun

• Add small plastic animals or people to your winter scene.

• Before you spray on the snow spray, add a small mirror to the center of your scene to make a pond.

• You can make a larger snow scene by using a larger lid.

You Will Need

a plastic lid (about 5 to 8 inches wide) • Sticky Dough • small pine cones • a can of snow spray

Sticky Dough

Mix a small amount of water with some flour until you can form a dough ball.

Tree Collage

Let your imagination go to work!

1. Cut a large piece of green paper into a triangle to make a simple tree shape.

2. Brush some glue onto a part of your tree and decorate it with scraps of colored paper, wrapping paper, and foil paper.

3. Continue until your whole tree is decorated.

For More Fun

• Brighten up your tree with scraps of ribbon or rickrack, buttons, puzzle pieces, stickers, and so on.

• Decorate smaller tree shapes and attach string to their tops to turn them into ornaments.

• Sprinkle glitter over your Tree Collage for a sparkly effect.

You Will Need

a large piece of green paper • scissors • glue • a brush • scraps of colored paper • scraps of wrapping paper • scraps of foil paper

Cookie Cutter Ornaments

1. Make a batch of Ornament Dough and divide it in half.

2. Rub some flour on a rolling pin and roll out the dough on a piece of waxed paper.

3. Use cookie cutters to cut out shapes and place them on a cookie sheet.

4. Use a straw to poke a hole in the top of each shape.

5. Let your ornaments air-dry for 1 to 2 days, or bake them at 300°F for 1 hour (longer if the dough is thick).

6. When your ornaments are dry and cool, paint them with tempera paint or enamel paint.

These are great as gifts for friends and family!

7. When the paint is dry, loop yarn through the holes at the tops of the ornaments so they can be hung on a tree.

For More Fun

• Sprinkle your ornaments with glitter before the paint dries.

You Will Need

Ornament Dough • flour • a rolling pin • waxed paper • holiday cookie cutters • a cookie sheet • a straw • paint • yarn

Ornament Dough

With a fork, stir together 2 cups flour, ½ cup salt and ¾ cup water until a ball forms. Place the dough on a floured surface and knead it for 2 to 3 minutes.

Glitter Ball

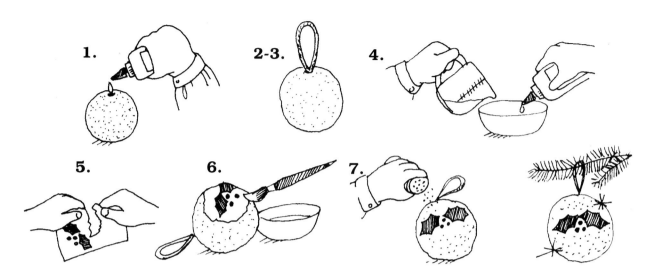

Brighten your holiday with this sparkly ornament!

1. Poke a small hole in a Styrofoam ball and fill the hole with glue.

2. Make a loop with a piece of yarn and poke both ends into the hole.

3. Let the glue dry.

4. Pour some glue into a small container and mix in an equal amount of water.

5. Carefully tear out a picture from a holiday napkin and place it on your ball.

6. Use a brush to completely cover the picture and the rest of the ball with glue.

7. While the glue is still damp, sprinkle clear glitter all over the ball and picture.

8. Hang the ornament up to dry.

You Will Need

a Styrofoam ball • glue • yarn • water • a holiday napkin • a brush • clear glitter

For More Fun

• You can also glue pictures and glitter to candles and glass containers. They make great gifts.

A Note to Parents and Teachers

The activities in this book have been written so that children in first, second, and third grades can follow most of the directions with minimal adult help.

The activities are also appropriate for 3- to 5-year-old children, who can easily do the activities with your help.

You may also wish to extend the learning opportunities in this book by discussing the life cycle of a tree, letting your children count or sort fall leaves, or having your children act out the story (there can be as many Ellies as you wish).

Children learn so much better when they can express their ideas and feelings through age-appropriate activities. We know you'll enjoy seeing your children's eyes light up when you extend a story with related activities.

Ellie, the Queen of the Ball

Sung to: "Up on the Housetop"

Ellie the Evergreen was sad in the fall,

While all of the other trees dressed for the ball.

Her gown was green from her feet to her head,

The other trees' gowns were gold and red.

    Ooh, ooh, ooh — everyone said.

    Ahh, ahh, ahh — gowns gold and red.

Ellie the Evergreen looked so sad,

While all of the other trees were oh, so glad.

Then came the winter and everything changed,

Ellie was now the center of things.

Her gown was covered with beautiful lights,

The other trees were bare and stayed out of sight.

    Ooh, ooh, ooh — everyone said.

    Ahh, ahh, ahh — lights gold and red.

Ellie the Evergreen stood proud and tall,

At last she was the queen of the ball!

Jean Warren